The Narnia Journal

Adapted from *The Chronicles of Narnia* by

C. S. LEWIS

Illustrated by Mary Collier

 HarperFestival®
A Division of HarperCollinsPublishers

THE CHRONICLES OF NARNIA

C. S. Lewis's classic books, *The Chronicles of Narnia*, have enchanted readers of all ages with their wonderful tales of Narnia, the magical land ruled by Aslan the Great Lion, where Talking Beasts, Giants, Centaurs, and Dwarves live, and fierce battles are fought between good and evil. C. S. Lewis wrote *The Chronicles of Narnia* when he was an adult, but even as a young boy he wrote stories, letters, and tales of fantasy and adventure. In *The Narnia Journal* you can record your own stories, thoughts, ideas, and important moments, while you share in the adventure and magic of Narnia all year round.

January

Below the dam, much lower down, was more ice, but instead of being smooth this was all frozen into the foamy and wavy shapes in which the water had been rushing along at the very moment when the frost came. And where the water had been trickling over and spurting through the dam there was now a glittering wall of icicles, as if the side of the dam had been covered all over with flowers and wreaths and festoons of the purest sugar.

—*The Lion, the Witch and the Wardrobe*

There was no denying it was a beast of a day. Overhead was a sunless sky, muffled in clouds that were heavy with snow; underfoot, a black frost; blowing over it, a wind that felt as if it would take your skin off.

—*The Silver Chair*

The Queen took from somewhere among her wrappings a very small bottle which looked as if it were made of copper. Then, holding out her arm, she let one drop fall from it onto the snow beside the sledge. Edmund saw the drop for a second in mid-air, shining like a diamond.

—*The Lion, the Witch and the Wardrobe*

Just below them a dam had been built across this river, and when they saw it everyone suddenly remembered that of course beavers are always making dams and felt quite sure that Mr. Beaver had made this one.

—*The Lion, the Witch and the Wardrobe*

February

But instead of finding himself stepping out into the spare room he found himself stepping out from the shadow of some thick dark fir trees into an open place in the middle of a wood.

There was crisp, dry snow under his feet and more snow lying on the branches of the trees. Overhead there was a pale blue sky, the sort of sky one sees on a fine winter day in the morning. Straight ahead of him he saw between the tree-trunks the sun, just rising, very red and clear.

—*The Lion, the Witch and the Wardrobe*

_____

_____

_____

_____

_____

_____

_____

_____

_____

_____

_____

_____

_____

_____

_____

_____

_____

In most places the snow was still hardly lying at all, for the wind kept catching it up off the ground in sheets and clouds, and hurling it in their faces.

—*The Silver Chair*

"The White Witch? Who is she?"

"Why, it is she that has got all Narnia under her thumb. It's she that makes it always winter. Always winter and never Christmas; think of that!"

—*The Lion, the Witch and the Wardrobe*

_____

_____

_____

_____

_____

_____

_____

_____

_____

_____

_____

_____

_____

_____

_____

Wherever the Robin alighted a little shower of snow would fall off the branch. Presently the clouds parted overhead and the winter sun came out and the snow all around them grew dazzlingly bright.

—*The Lion, the Witch and the Wardrobe*

March

Every moment the patches of green grew
bigger and the patches of snow grew smaller.
Every moment more and more of the trees
shook off their robes of snow. Soon, wherever
you looked, instead of white shapes you saw
the dark green of firs or the black prickly
branches of bare oaks and beeches and elms.
Then the mist turned from white to gold and
presently cleared away altogether. Shafts of
delicious sunlight struck down onto the forest
floor and overhead you could see a blue sky
between the tree tops.

—*The Lion, the Witch and the Wardrobe*

It was good, springy ground for walking, and a day of pale winter sunlight.

—*The Silver Chair*

When next morning came there was a steady rain falling, so thick that when you looked out of the window you could see neither the mountains nor the woods nor even the stream in the garden.

—*The Lion, the Witch and the Wardrobe*

The waterfall keeps the Pool always dancing and bubbling and churning round and round as if it were on the boil, and that of course is how it got its name of Caldron Pool. It is liveliest in the early spring when the waterfall is swollen with all the snow that has melted off the mountains from up beyond Narnia in the Western Wild from which the river comes.

—*The Last Battle*

April

He noticed a dozen crocuses growing round the foot of an old tree—gold and purple and white. Then came a sound even more delicious than the sound of the water. Close beside the path they were following a bird suddenly chirped from the branch of a tree. It was answered by the chuckle of another bird a little further off. And then, as if that had been a signal, there was chattering and chirruping in every direction, and then a moment of full song, and within five minutes the whole wood was ringing with birds' music.

—*The Lion, the Witch and the Ward*

It was the first really warm day of that spring. The young leaves seemed to be much further out than yesterday: the snow-drops were over, but they saw several primroses.

—*The Last Battle*

And then she would go on deck and take a look from the forecastle at a sea that was a brighter blue each morning and drink in an air that was a little warmer day by day.

—*The Voyage of the* Dawn Treader

There was no trace of the fog now. The sky became bluer and bluer, and now there were white clouds hurrying across it from time to time.

—*The Lion, the Witch and the Wardrobe*

May

All of them passed in through the golden gates, into the delicious smell that blew toward them out of that garden and into the cool mixture of sunlight and shadow under the trees, walking on springy turf that was all dotted with white flowers.

—*The Last Battle*

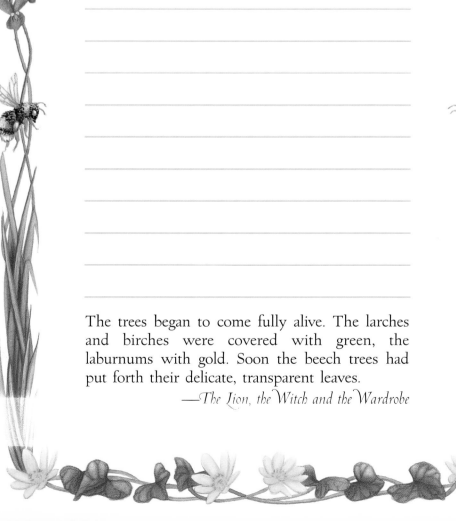

The trees began to come fully alive. The larches and birches were covered with green, the laburnums with gold. Soon the beech trees had put forth their delicate, transparent leaves.

—*The Lion, the Witch and the Wardrobe*

The eastern sky changed from white to pink and from pink to gold. The Voice rose and rose, till all the air was shaking with it. And just as it swelled to the mightiest and most glorious sound it had yet produced, the sun arose.

—*The Magician's Nephew*

Digory had never seen such a sun. You could imagine that it laughed for joy as it came up.

—*The Magician's Nephew*

June

All Narnia, many-colored with lawns and rocks and heather and different sorts of trees, lay spread out below them, the river winding through it like a ribbon of quicksilver. They could already see over the tops of the low hills which lay northward on their right; beyond those hills a great moorland sloped gently up and up to the horizon. On their left the mountains were much higher, but every now and then there was a gap when you could see, between steep pine woods, a glimpse of the southern lands that lay beyond them, looking blue and far away.

—*The Magician's Nephew*

_____

_____

_____

_____

_____

_____

_____

_____

_____

_____

_____

_____

_____

_____

_____

_____

_____

_____

The water was not bitingly cold as all of them (and especially Puzzle) expected, but of a delicious foamy coolness.

—*The Last Battle*

The valley itself, with its brown, cool river, and grass and moss and wild flowers and rhododendrons, was such a pleasant place that it made you want to ride slowly.

—*The Horse and His Boy*

A heavenly smell, warm and golden, as if from all
the most delicious fruits and flowers of the world,
was coming up to them from somewhere ahead.

—*The Magician's Nephew*

July

Before them the turf, dotted with white flowers, sloped down to the brow of a cliff. Far below them, so that the sound of the breaking waves was very faint, lay the sea. Shasta had never seen it from such a height and never seen so much of it before, nor dreamed how many colors it had. On either hand the coast stretched away, headland after headland, and at the points you could see the white foam running up the rocks but making no noise because it was so far off. There were gulls flying overhead and the heat shivered on the ground; it was a blazing day.

—*The Horse and His Boy*

All the light was green light that came through the leaves: but there must have been a very strong sun overhead, for this green daylight was bright and warm.

—*The Magician's Nephew*

They all now waded back and went first across the smooth, wet sand and then up to the dry, crumbly sand that sticks to one's toes, and began putting on their shoes and socks.

—*Prince Caspian*

There was no land in sight and no clouds in the sky. The sun was about where it ought to be at ten o'clock in the morning, and the sea was a dazzling blue.

—*Prince Caspian*

August

For an afternoon's ramble ending in a picnic
tea it would have been delightful. It had
everything you could want on an occasion of
that sort—rumbling waterfalls, silver cascades,
deep, amber-colored pools, mossy rocks, and
deep moss on the banks in which you could
sink over your ankles.

—*Prince Caspian*

_____

_____

_____

_____

_____

_____

_____

_____

_____

_____

_____

_____

_____

_____

"There's no hurry," said Digory with a huge yawn.

"I think there is," said Polly. "This place is too quiet. It's so—so dreamy. You're almost asleep. If we once give in to it we shall just lie down and drowse forever and ever."

—*The Magician's Nephew*

Palm trees and pillared arcades cast shadows over the burning pavements. And through the arched gateways of many a palace Shasta caught sight of green branches, cool fountains, and smooth lawns.

—*The Horse and His Boy*

_____

_____

_____

_____

_____

_____

_____

_____

_____

_____

_____

_____

_____

_____

Shasta, very thirsty, sat up and rubbed his eyes. The desert was blindingly white and, though there was a murmur of noises from the city behind him, where he sat everything was perfectly still.

—*The Horse and His Boy*

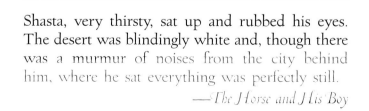

September

And in the evening if it turned chilly, as it sometimes did after the heavy rains, he was a comfort to everyone, for the whole party would come and sit with their backs against his hot sides and get well warmed and dried; and one puff of his fiery breath would light the most obstinate fire.

—*The Voyage of the* Dawn Treader

Now all four of them were sitting on a seat at a railway station with trunks and playboxes piled up round them. They were, in fact, on their way back to school.

—*Prince Caspian*

For the sun sank lower and lower till the western sky was all like one great furnace full of melted gold; and it set at last behind a jagged peak which stood up against the brightness as sharp and flat as if it were cut out of cardboard.

—*The Magician's Nephew*

At the same moment an exercise book which had been lying beside Edmund on the bed flapped, rose and sailed through the air to the wall behind him, and Lucy felt all her hair whipping round her face as it does on a windy day.

—*The Voyage of the* Dawn Treader

October

"In Harfang you may or may not hear tidings of the City Ruinous, but certainly you shall find good lodgings and merry hosts. You would be wise to winter there, or, at the least, to tarry certain days for your ease and refreshment. There you shall have steaming baths, soft beds, and bright hearths; and the roast and the baked and the sweet and the strong will be on the table four times a day."

—*The Silver Chair*

Rynelf returned with the spiced wine steaming in
a flagon and four silver cups. It was just what one
wanted, and as Lucy and Edmund sipped it they
could feel the warmth going right down to their toes.

—The Voyage of the Dawn Treader

The big snowy mountains rose above them in every direction. The valleys, far beneath them, were so green, and all the streams which tumbled down from the glaciers into the main river were so blue, that it was like flying over gigantic pieces of jewelry.

—*The Magician's Nephew*

Immediately the sky became full of shooting stars.
Even one shooting star is a fine thing to see; but
these were dozens, and then scores, and then
hundreds, till it was like silver rain: and it went
on and on.

—*The Last Battle*

November

Eastward the flat marsh stretched to low sand-hills on the horizon, and you could tell by the salt tang in the wind which blew from that direction that the sea lay over there. To the North there were low pale-colored hills, in places bastioned with rock. The rest was all flat marsh. It would have been a depressing place on a wet evening. Seen under a morning sun, with a fresh wind blowing, and the air filled with the crying of birds, there was something fine and fresh and clean about its loneliness.

—The Silver Chair

At either side of it were many chairs of stone richly carved and with silken cushions upon the seats. But on the table itself there was set out such a banquet as had never been seen.

— *The Voyage of the Dawn Treader*

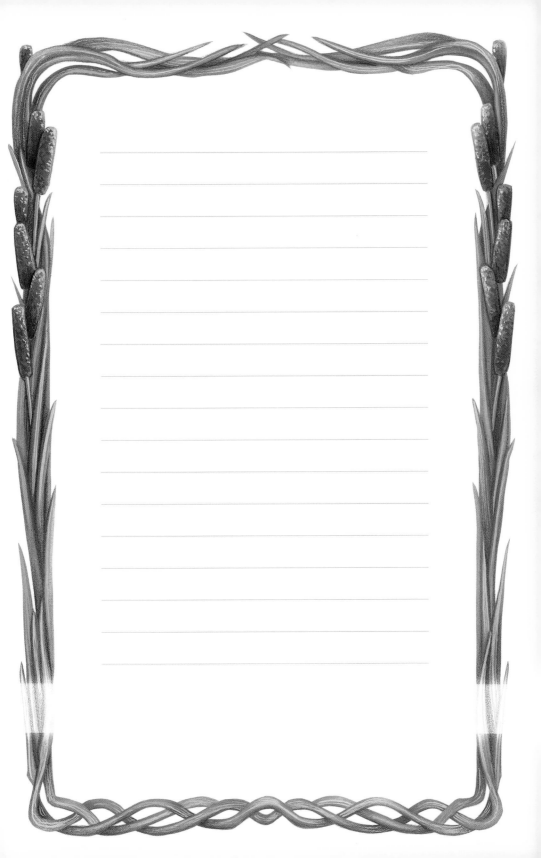

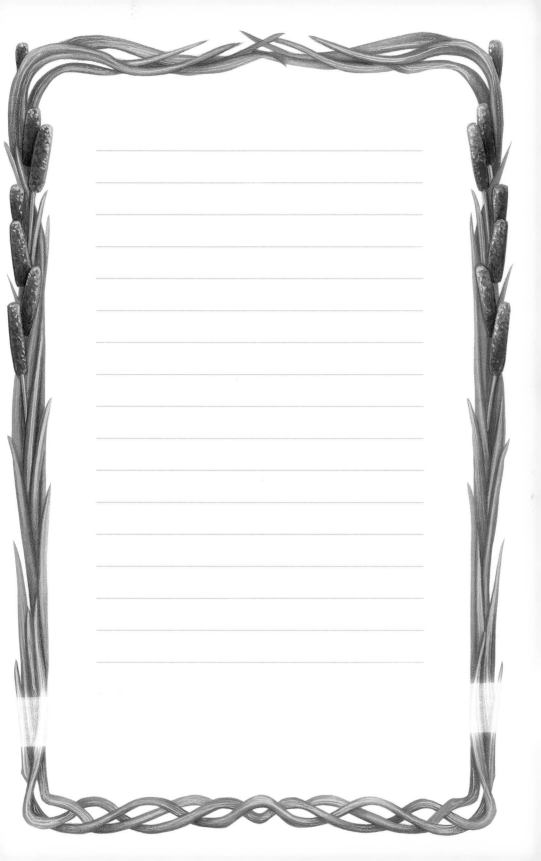

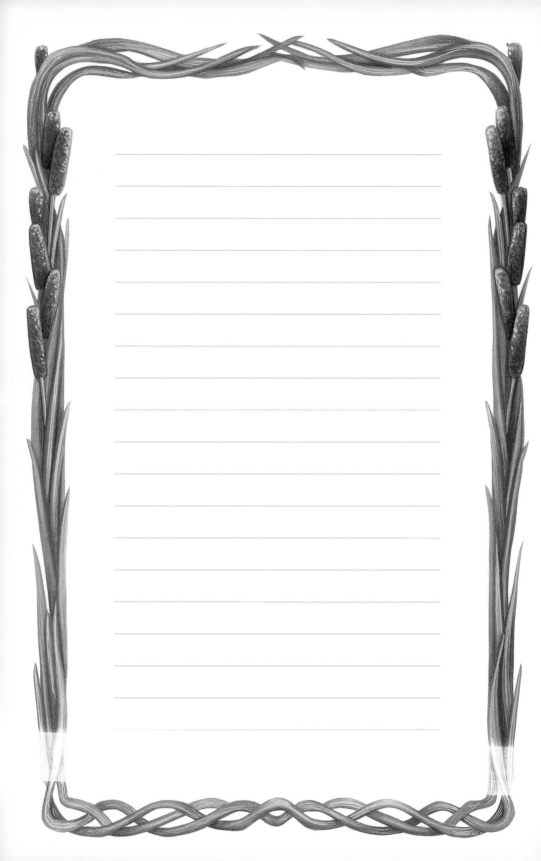

They were on a great flat plain which was cut into countless little islands by countless channels of water. The islands were covered with coarse grass and bordered with reeds and rushes.

—*The Silver Chair*

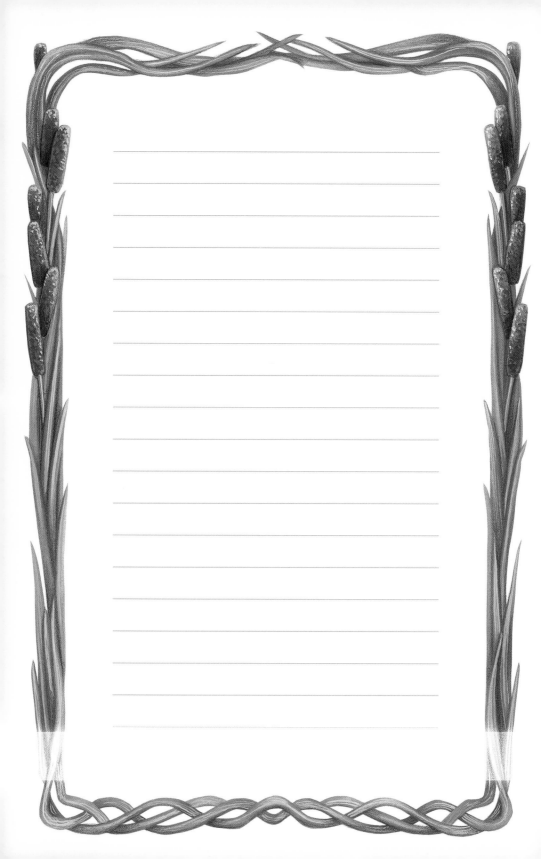

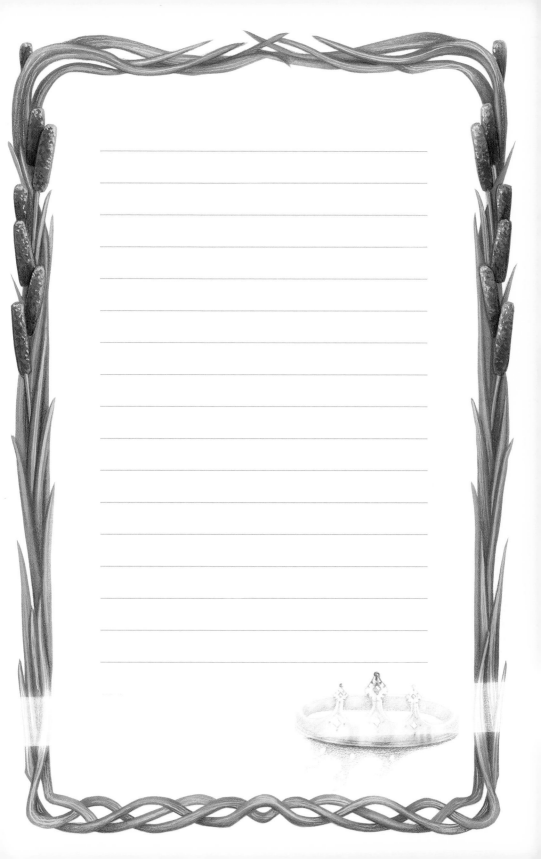

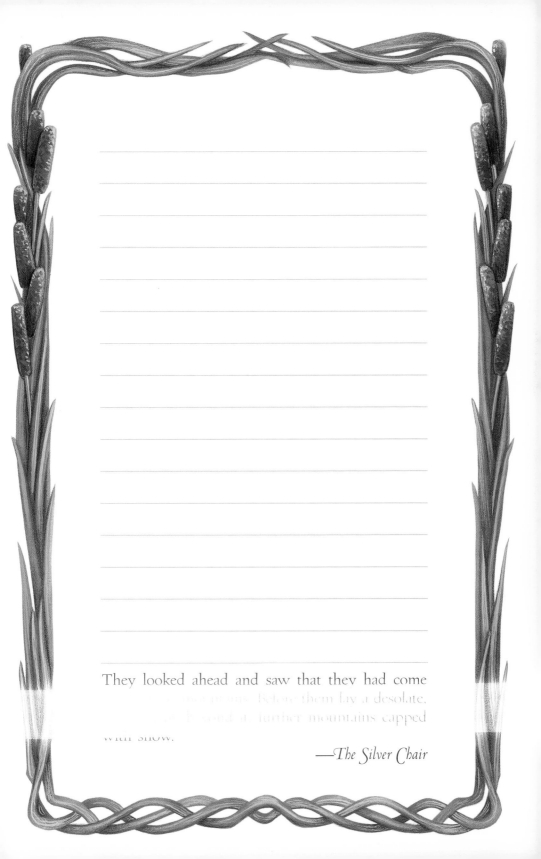

They looked ahead and saw that they had come

with snow.

—*The Silver Chair*

December

He brought out (I suppose from the big bag at his back, but nobody quite saw him do it) a large tray containing five cups and saucers, a bowl of lump sugar, a jug of cream, and a great big teapot all sizzling and piping hot. Then he cried out "Merry Christmas! Long live the true King!" and cracked his whip, and he and the reindeer and the sledge and all were out of sight before anyone realized that they had started.

—*The Lion, the Witch and the Wardrobe*

Something cold and soft was falling on her. A moment later she found that she was standing in the middle of a wood at night-time with snow under her feet and snowflakes falling through the air.

—*The Lion, the Witch and the Wardrobe*

On the sledge sat a person whom everyone knew the moment they set eyes on him. He was a huge man in a bright red robe (bright as hollyberries) with a hood that had fur inside it and a great white beard that fell like a foamy waterfall over his chest.

—*The Lion, the Witch and the Wardrobe*

"I've come at last," said he. "She has kept me out
for a long time, but I have got in at last. Aslan is
on the move. The Witch's magic is weakening."
—*The Lion, the Witch and the Wardrobe*